Caught in the Myth

Previous Books by Alison Stone

Dazzle
Ordinary Magic
Dangerous Enough
They Sing at Midnight
Masterplan (collaborative poems with Eric Greinke)
Guzzle (chapbook)
Borrowed Logic (chapbook)
From the Fool to the World (chapbook)

Caught in the Myth

by

Alison Stone

The New York Quarterly Foundation, Inc.
Beacon, New York

NYQ Books™ is an imprint of The New York Quarterly Foundation, Inc.

The New York Quarterly Foundation, Inc.
P. O. Box 470
Beacon, NY 12508

www.nyq.org

First Edition

Set in New Baskerville

Layout and Design by Raymond P. Hammond

Front Cover Painting by Alison Stone

Author Photograph by Alison Stone

Library of Congress Control Number: 2019947590

ISBN: 978-1-63045-060-1

For My Father

Acknowledgments

Poems in this book, some in earlier versions, have appeared in the following publications:

Art Times: Arachne; Marble Portrait Bust of a Young Man; Caligula; Hadrian; Marble Portrait of a Man (originally identified as Julius Caesar)
Bad Pony: Once Upon a Time
Big Scream: After the Mountains, More Mountains
The Comstock Review: Sorry, Perseus
Descant: Endymion, Sisyphus
First of the Month: Frozen Part 3; Reeva Steenkamp; Gabby Douglas, "Rape on Campuses isn't Always Because People are Rapists;" Thirteen-Year-Old Girl Kills Herself after Father Posts Shaming Video; Ivanka Trump's Body; Though if I Hurt Myself Doing it, at least I Still have Health Insurance; Report (under the title Forbidden)
Forge: Frozen
Folio: Acteon's Hounds
Madness Muse Press: Alcoholic Cento
Michigan Quarterly Review: Pandora
The Mom Egg Review: Filling the Eggs
Pink Panther: Cinderella, Erysichthon's Daughter, Mary Magdalene
Poetry Daily: Pandora
Poetry International: Prom Night
Prachya Review: Judith, Jezebel, Wounded Amazon
Red Rock Review: Hercules
Stone Canoe: Reserves, A Dainaid Sets the Record Straight
Three Drops from a Cauldron (Beltane Special): Easter

Heretic appeared in the anthology, *Alongside We Travel: Contemporary Poets on Autism,* edited by Sean Thomas Dougherty (NYQ Books, 2019)

Thanks to:

Members of The Poets' Circle and One O'clock Poets, for feedback on earlier versions.

Raymond Hammond, for believing in this book.

LitSpace St. Pete, for a residency that gave me time and space to work on this and other projects.

Faye Rapoport DesPres, for inspiring friendship and insightful comments.

Jennifer Magidson, for friendship then and now. And for Rome.

My family, for understanding the time and commitment this takes.

Contents

These things never happened, but always are.

—*Sallustio, Degli Dei e del Mondo IIV*

Arachne

Every story starts
in the body.

A need felt.
Filled

or thwarted.
Pushed from the belly,

passions
string themselves out.

Lies unspool
their sticky silk.

Warp, woof,
the crisscrossing threads

of betrayal. Intricate
patterns of loss.

Who can turn away?
Caught in the myth's weave,

the listener—immobile,
rapt.

Mythology

At the center, a woman—
comely nymph or princess,
or ugly, and therefore evil.
Also desire, for love or sex

with a comely nymph or princess.
There must be obstacles
to this desire for love or sex,
or for beauty, which equals love.

There must be obstacles—
villains or vengeful gods
inflamed by beauty, which equals love.
And a body of water,

crossed by villains or vengeful gods.
Something is dropped in, or pulled out
from the body of water.
The story ends neatly, though often in grief.

Something is dropped in or pulled out
of an old well or an enchanted bag.
The story ends neatly, though often in grief.
These tales teach us about ourselves.

An enchanted well is guarded by an old bag,
ugly, therefore evil.
In these tales that teach us about ourselves,
at the center, there's a woman.

Athena

Mother love is the first love.

    My heart
             broken at birth.

Where did I get my grey eyes?

Never suckled,
        never sung to sleep, I was given

             armor, olive groves.

And wisdom, that dry consolation prize.

Father swelled—a child
          wholly his.

      Eternal daddy's girl.

He let me hold his weapons.

      Let me live.

Never courted, never wife.

      Golden bridle
         for the winged horse of desire.

armor   olive   wisdom   stifled cry

Mother-wound
      the first wound.

Grim

Wanting fairness in her fairy tales,
my daughter's mad at Jack, who breaks
and enters, then steals
not only treasure but the giant's pet.
*What if someone climbs in and takes
Merlin?* She vises an arm around our shelter
cat. Jack's poor, starving mother
doesn't sway her. Wrong is wrong.

Life is clear at five, indisputable as flowers
or a shove, before we learn to gnaw the gristle
of compromise and call it nourishing,
before we hone our lies. A time we're still
awake enough to enter the heart
of the goose, carried roughly from home
and forced to lay for strangers
who don't know or care
which nest-straw she prefers,
her favorite food, her name.

Erysichthon's Daughter

I knew what was coming.
He'd pawned the stereo, sold
Mama's rings. Slave
to the twist in his guts,

the insatiable craving.
What chance did love have?
Seen through pain-mad eyes,
I wasn't even real.

The first one was a fisherman—sour
beard, wide-knuckled hands.
I left my body behind.
Again and again Father sold me,

stuffing the cash in his coat
and rushing off to feed,
while I prayed myself
into a mare or bird.

Each time I swore
would be the last.
I heard the ocean's call,
planned to leave at dawn.

I couldn't run.
Daughter-training tethered me,
my devotion limitless
and futile as his struggle to be full.

Ivanka Trump's Body

isn't hers
>How could it be?

Raw gnawing hunger
>>to acquire

shiny objects

>a gold toilet   a daughter

He brags about
>her large breasts,
>>repeats how he'd "like to..."

His eyes closed
>as he kisses her mouth
His hands
>squeezing her hips at the convention

>Why is her mother silent?

Howard Stern asks, can he
>call her "a piece of ass"

Hesitation
>(He is, after all, a father)

>*Yeah*

Midas

What's remembered is the lesson—
greed's enslavement, craving
followed to ruin. The fact
that grabbing hands spoil
all they touch. Food turned
cold and useless in my mouth.
How, docile as a beaten child,
I begged to return the gift.

Most don't understand
my emptiness—the core
of me untouchable, as though
my heart, sore and wanting,
beat behind glass.
Longing for someone
to break in.

Why could no one
know me?
My simple wife content
to love a stranger, my daughter
imagining the husk before her
was her dad.

Resigned, I vowed—
If my life can be no more
than surface,
let each surface shine.

Tales omit the rapture
of those first bright hours.
Virile with fulfillment,
I reached out for everything.
Belly full,
my daughter elsewhere, safe.
I, a god, transforming
this unsatisfying world
to endless dazzle.

Thirteen-Year-Old Girl Kills Herself after Father Posts Shaming Video

I can't wipe from my mind
your blank face, features delicate
even in the grainy footage,
your hacked hair (not shaved, at least
he spared you that) actually punk-cute,
though of course that's irrelevant.

What he took from you was choice,
control of the figuring-itself-out self
you show the world. You couldn't know
bullies weaken from the years
that would have set you free.

For you, each day held
steel against your nape, humiliation
always just a click away, nothing
left to do but jump.

After the camera pans to a pile
of your shorn locks, his self-righteous
voice asks, *Was it worth it?*
Your one whispered syllable's
the same answer you gave the world
whose beauty offered, *Stay.*

Bust of a Girl

Nose smashed, lips lopsided,
your bruised face could belong to
too many contemporary women,
broken and owned.

Even in imagined wholeness—
chips smoothed over, missing
parts returned—sadness
leaks from you like wine
from a cracked urn.

Perhaps pain flowed
from the sculptor's fingers—
the sorrow of a wife
lost in childbirth
or a son felled by war.

Was some specific grief
captured in stone,
or does your battered mouth tell
broader truth?
                    At the market, fat flies
                    hover near the stalls
                    with sweetest meat.
                    Behind the ruler's olive groves
                    sprawl fields of asphodel.

Easter

This is not my myth—
a resurrected savior
glimpsed strolling through town
like a celebrity.
I prefer the stories they stole from—
Dionysus felled and risen,
Ostara with Her sacred hare.

Anyone who's thrown dirt
on a loved one's coffin knows
that coming back's a fairy tale,
though metaphor makes its case—
flowers' color-rich unfurling,
the old dog leaping
for a stick. My daughter
smiling with my mother's mouth.

Filling the Eggs

Though it's the hunt that delights them,
I place stickers, candy, glitter hair ties
in the plastic shells.
An even number, inked
with their initials to prevent squabbles.

My lastborn wants a younger sibling.
Otherwise I'll never have
someone to boss around. She doesn't understand
how a woman's body winds down,
or hear, when I stand up, my joints
make noises like a closing door.

I watch from the porch as my daughters
forage through the flowerbeds in filmy
dresses, a tumult of blossoms
beneath their eager hands.
Their baskets loaded with eggs.

Self-Portrait as Demeter, Tricked

I wake to snow
over the new spring flowers,
ice-cased hyacinth, daffodils'
bent necks. Relief from a storm-filled
winter short-lived as the calm
between boy drama and the fever
my daughter rises with, clutching my hand
and muttering, *Be quiet, birds,* and
Too much light. Not cold cloths
or stories, nothing soothes her as she burns
between this quilt-covered bed
and some other world.

Sisyphus

Everyone knows the boulder,
the torture of eternal, pointless pushing,
then the inevitable downhill roll.
Few remember the reason—Death
tricked, fifty extra years to savor
olive bread beneath the Tuscan sun,
fifty cakes whose flames
were his to snuff.

For a chance at six more months,
my mother offered her body
to the surgeon's knife, made her chest
a port for the delivery of drugs
that left her dizzy, bone-thin.

We call cancer patients brave,
but really it's the dumb animal drive
to live, even life reduced
to a schedule of painkillers
and broth. When we imagine Sisyphus,

looking almost alive as his muscles knot
with strain, each foot pushing off the dirt,
we realize that the rock's bulk
and the ache in his broad back are reminders
of the virile man he was, and also that he's
free to return in memory to boyhood games
or his wife's soft skin. (He must have consciousness;
without it, there's no point to punishment.)

If my mother had angered the gods,
or at least the deity she believed in,
would she have been sentenced
to an infinite, repetitive task? Her post-death body
strong enough to accomplish it, her mind still hers—

perhaps remembering her honeymoon, or smiling
at our private jokes. Maybe hearing
news about her grandchildren from a new shade.

Instead, my mother
lived unselfishly, followed rules,
and is gone.

After the Mountains, More Mountains

What use are proverbs
to the afflicted? The mountain's
pocked face greets my dog and me
each morning. An hour's easy climb
to the first peak. My friend
whose liver failed
raised enough money to fly
for a transplant at a famous clinic,
was told on arrival that they'd
changed their minds.
She lies on the floor
much of the day, walks a bit,
writes when she can.
My daughter hands me a homemade sun,
stained the crimson of first or last light.
I lift it toward the painted puffs
of cloud on her ceiling, tilt
so sparkles blaze. Stray
glitter gilds my palm.
I say *gratitude*,
mean *fear of loss*.

Damocles Undergoes Treatment

Doctors can cure
everything these days.
The hair snipped carefully,
sword tamed
to a glass-cased souvenir,
a conversation piece.

My room looks monochrome
without the shadow
of its blade. Who am I if not a man
in peril, my cup filled
with sympathy? What can
I accomplish that will satisfy
like that endangered life, when getting
through the day was luck enough?

Judith

No yen for battle, no bloodlust.
I even looked away when they butchered the lambs.
Still, my village gray with dust, our crops
dying like prayer
in the earth's parched throat.
A woman does what she must.

As I swayed past him,
Holophernes grinned.
Shrewd general,
but passion's fool.

My weapons—kohl
around the eyes, crushed beetles
to redden my lips. The axe
blade sharp as thirst.

Two strokes—one for
the blocked river, one to sever
the last stubborn flap.

Stuck on the gate, his head
issued silent commands.
The soldiers rushed away like water
dammed, then freed.

Actaeon's Hounds

Fur, hooves, antlers didn't fool us—
we knew his scent at once,
its undertones of arrogance
and wine. Years we chased
game for him in all weather,
paws bleeding from brambles, and not one
Good boy or scratch behind the ears.
If the prey escaped, he drove
his boot into our bellies, our soft snouts.
He never even gave us names.
When we smelled his fear, the wolf
inside us triumphed. His flesh
opened like a kennel door.

Pagan

What kind of god creates a world
and asks us to show love for him
by turning away from its brightness?
To trade wine, lips, rock 'n roll
for an idea of light?
Why not put the bible down
and start devouring?
We'll break into pieces either way.
For the brief time that we have
these bodies, let's adore them.

Jezebel

Always one religion
devours another,
always the new god
hungry for blood.

The truth
of any prophecy's decided
by those left alive.

Sure I painted my face,
though beauty failed
to stop the eunuchs'
grabbing hands.

Tossed from the balcony,
I plummeted.
They cheered to see my body
broken like a law,
my flesh manna
to the ravenous pack.

Vashti

I'll obey your order—
shake my booty,
sway my naked hips
until the drunk guests moan.
I know what a woman's body's for.

But not alone.
Husband, drop your robe
and join me, your lined skin
and paunch becoming handsome
as we move together in love's light.
Take my hand and start to shimmy.
Then I'll dance.

Mary Magdalene

I had accepted death, understood
weak men revile what they crave,
how shame can be pushed
into another's body the way a spear enters
the side of a boar.

The men who had known me
stood in front, stones raised.
They would have splashed
my brains across the road,
then gone home and kissed their wives.

He came. Rescued and blessed me.
Then he left.

In my dreams,
his hands.

In the morning,
sun on my solitary body, I tighten
my cloak against the villagers' stares.
I've never felt so naked.

They say love heals.
First, it shows what's broken.

Covenant

Chosen People is both honor
and duty, my teacher repeats,
the obligation to snuff the small
self in piety's service,
to carry laws like sacks of lucky rocks.
So when the cantor's hands wander
in his locked office,
I cooperate. I want to.
Not for pleasure, my frozen body
dumb as an idol, but to be plucked
from the pack of untouched,
nondescript girls. For the heft
of specialness. Being chosen.

Watching *The Ten Commandments*

I'd forgotten all the sex—
tight costumes, machinations and murder
for lust's sake, the busty princess moaning,
Moses, Moses like a soap opera queen.

The dead firstborns had marked
my young mind, the ocean pulled back
like a curtain, fear
in the drowning horses' eyes.

Mostly I remembered
a toddler reaching for Pharaoh's jewels,
an angel forcing his hand
to the coal, his burned tongue.

Except that scene's not in the movie.
No speech impediment for Heston's
smooth-talking savior. I must have
stuck it in from stories heard or read,

though part of me would swear
the tape's been edited and it once played
between the basket on the river
and the slave's shawl trapped by rock.

Imagination trumps fact every time,
the way Heston's staff-turned-serpent
swallowed Brenner's. Our memories
stubborn and untrustworthy as any god.

Demosthenes

Tongue trained to dance
around a mouth of rock,
I rehearsed while running, pit
my lungs against the shouting
of the sea. Practiced until
I commanded language
as the moon enslaves the waves.

Each word can be a kiss.
A coin. A slap.
Pointed sentences
rouse sleeping politicians;
the right spray of syllables
cleans slander
from a just man's name.

Hear me, citizens,
before the tyrant's armies
march. While the vessel is safe
is the time for everyone
to show his zeal.

Citizens, you fail
to listen, swat
my words away like gnats.
Heed before time
proves my warnings true.

Once the sea
has overwhelmed the vessel,
zeal is useless.

Statue of Caracalla

One son dies
in his mother's arms. The other
watches soldiers fill their bags.
The first wife falls with a soft *oh.*

History needs a villain,
says the stone.

Rome is an animal
on its back.
Silver taken from her coins
mirrors the moon's veiled face.

Remember, says the brother's ghost,
the way we played at war
with wooden swords?

I dabbed perfume on my breasts
to please you, whispers
the dead bride. The new citizens
bleed taxes. Well-paid soldiers
shine their knives.

Build, says the brother's ghost,
a bath immense enough
to wash you clean.

Ambush near the moon-god's shrine.
A husband's blood
to match my dress, croons the bride.

Once I was uncarved stone,
says the stone.
Now I'm an emperor
who drank and sang with soldiers.

I'm still the moon,
says the moon.

40

Endymion

Life can't compete.
Why trade lush dreams
for labor, moon-kisses
for the frustrations and fading
of ordinary love?
Neighbors see me spellbound,
sprawled. They click their tongues,
sigh, *Shame* and *Such a handsome boy.*
My parents beg priests
and physicians for a cure.
They don't understand
I'm care-less. Free. Cool
soil soft against my skin. All
striving gone. Every night the silver
lady with her hands of light.

Report

The waning moon makes me feel *vulnerable,*
like watching a woman
with a slice carved from her side.

The American moon's *transgender,*
formerly the German moon-god,
their sun-goddess's spouse.

Flaming and fabulous,
our Mr. Sun dazzles in *science-based*
hot pink and fuchsia scarves.

What sense of *entitlement* lets me
dilly dally, skygazing,
lost in the *diversity* of myth,

dumb as a *fetus*
to procrastination's many
evidence-based ills?

Marble Portrait of a Man (originally identified as Julius Caesar)

No fame, no venerated name.
No gold-bloated purse. No army
honored to die for my whim.
I'm a nobody, only notable
for the broad forehead, narrow chin,
and long, scrawny neck that mirror
his face more closely
than any blood kin.

Play up the resemblance,
I ordered, and the artist
did his work so well,
no viewer can be certain
if the sculpture shimmers
with my own or borrowed light.

Marble Portrait Bust of a Young Man

Your nose is missing, proof
that what we put out into the world
is most vulnerable. Still, what remains
proves your good looks.
Perhaps you were a noble, modeling
for vanity's sake. Or maybe poor,
grateful for the coins your face could earn.

What happened after
you posed? Did you die
decades later, surrounded by family?
Or were you snuffed in youth
by a rival whose wife's eyes
lingered too long on your strong jaw,
your pretty lips?

Co-Emperor Lucius Verus

Our true mother was Rome.
We suckled sour milk,
lived for her whims.

It took two adoptions,
two broken betrothals,
and the loyalty of a brother
with no shared blood
to put me on the throne.

What is a family?

Lesser of equals, I sprinkled
gold dust in my hair
to try and shine. I was good
with words, pleased people
with my lack of pomp; but my reign
was marked with blood.
Always some province at war. Always
some brash cad who thought he should rule.
Men falling over each other like cubs.

History can't decide—was I
a debauched dandy who partied
on his way to battle
and missed the action, or a strategist,
wise enough to send the best generals?

No one disputes that I found love,
my Panthea ravishing and witty,
her voice like the fall of rain.
Marcus made me marry
his daughter.

Did I die from smallpox, spoiled
meat, a stroke?

A half-heard phrase, a question mark,
I ended how I lived.

When the pack is short of food,
a wolf will eat her young.

Ambition

Fame's the beast you track
through swamps as thick
mud tries to suck you under. Fame
the flame that burns thin
skin, the sunlight
shining on your brother's toothy
grin as he dangles a snake
on top of you, small you,
crouched in shadow, bouncing a cracked
rubber ball and dropping jacks.

Emperor Augustus

My father is a memory—
shiny boots, thick fingers closing
over my four-year-old fist.
My son is a broken wish.

Partners are milk.
I'm cream.
Three turns to two. Then one.
Rome's mine.

See my magician's trick
of giving power to the senators
and taking it back when they blink.
Now I'm divine.

No heir? I'll sever
happy marriages to make one,
easily as gods rhyme *child*
with *blood.*

What more
could a ruler want?
In dreams I trace the edges
of my empire,

show its splendors
to the proud
shades of my father,
my young son.

Domitian

Remember, Father, how you pried
my fingers from your sleeve?

Raised by strangers, touched
only by Mother's ghost, I lost

myself in art and books.
Recited poems by heart

imagining you listened.
Can a father love only one son?

You shared jokes and the empire
with Titus, gave me petty titles

the way grown-ups entertain a toddler
with a wooden sword.

If I left him feverish and failing,
ran to claim my crown,

how can you blame me?
Finally the chance

to prove myself a man.
I hobbled the aristocrats,

hovered over every part of Roman life.
A proper patriarch's involved.

Surely, Father, you can understand—
I became what I craved.

Father, in my dream
Minerva turned her back,

left me to die.
Or was that you?

Though senators would legislate
my name into oblivion—

coins and statues melted, arches smashed—
as daggers spilled our shared blood,

my last thought was
had I done enough to make you proud?

Hercules

Monsters are easy.
Child's play to squeeze a snake
into limp rope, to shoulder
the world's weight.

Fools call me a hero, fail
to see my drunken stumbling,
the blood in my wake.

I walk under a sky dark
as my dead wife's eyes and know
there is no punishment
severe enough to scour me clean.

The river's cold, slick surface
mirrors back the only beast
I couldn't slay or master.

Zeus Ammon

Humans try to make me
in their image, murmur
prayers and lies from
the same side of their mouths.

Their myths show the appeal
of vengeance, prove how many
long to cheat on their wives.

Why do they mash me up
with Egypt's Big Guy?
Stick horns on my head
like a tacky hat?

I am that I am
and need no man
to name me God.

Hermes

When I was born, the bright world
flicked its many tails.
Cows' eyes, deep ponds
of placidness. How could I not
abscond with such lovely mooing?

I gave back other music—
saw a tortoise sunning on a rock
and knew that notes from holes
drilled in its shell
would hold the listener spellbound.

Guide of heroes,
loved by gods and living humans
for my quick delivery,
go-between in dramas
more compelling than any play,
I only drag my feet when leading down
the slow souls of the dead.

Marciana

Bath-damp curls and chubby
baby limbs—how could I not adore
this tiny sidekick, loyal fan?
I fussed over and bossed him.

Eager to please, he threw himself
into whatever game I fancied, acted
out the slow, devoted pupil (I played
teacher); I an empress, he, the faithful horse.

When he learned the truth—
that boys have power,
girls have none, he loved me
so much, he pretended not to know.

I moved in with him, took his wife
as sister. He took my advice,
named me Augusta, hired the most skillful
artists to immortalize my face.

I was respected. Gave my all
to a supporting role.
Still, I never led an army,
never signed my name to a decree.

See the tightness of my lips,
my towering, hard hair
a substitute for monuments
I had no chance to build.

Prom Night

I. The Queen

Tonight is mine and perfect.
I can refuse to see that even rainbowed with streamers
the gym is sweaty and small, air thick with caste.
Misfits leaning against walls are cut by
smiles of the princesses in ruffled dresses
shuffling in circles, girls who kiss mauve
onto napkins inked with *Memories to last a lifetime,*
wondering if they should give it up
to slick-haired jocks who spike the punch
and hopefully finger motel keys.
This is my kingdom. I will never be so free
and beautiful again. I'm not smart enough
for college but I'm smart enough to know that years
and babies will thicken my waist and take the glow from my hair.
Let me dance before I'm swallowed
by this town. Tonight is all there is so when Ted pushes me
into the back and croaks, *Oh baby please,*
it hurts so bad, when he shoves into me,
I tell myself it's love, and I agree
to blow him while I wear my rhinestone crown.

II. The Rebel

Who needs some lame high school dance?
I hitch to the city, meet the crowd
at The Cramps, then head to Anne's.
We all ignore the explosion
of dishes and clothes. Arthur plays guitar.
Mark slaps rhythm on a frying pan,
warbling off-key, *Jesus died for somebody's sins but not mine.*
We hope Anne's drunk mother won't barge in and scream.
I'm here because I trust desire,
because I will follow my body anywhere, because I believe
that longing is a form of prayer.

I swallow the beauty
Johnny places on my tongue.
I'm dealing now, he crows, proud as a quarterback.
As couples stake out space under blankets,
I let Mark's friend Mick, or Nick,
put his hand up my skirt. Tell myself I'm free.
Sunlight leaks in through the window.
Paul spills beer and one of us will sit in it.

Hadrian

Little soul, you who will now
go off to places pale and barren, tell me—
how's a man's life measured? Do I pass?

I modeled discipline, killed
skillfully, ruled well.
Kept Rome in splendor. Walls fortified,
tall arches gleaming.
Half the world
improved and beautified.
The Jewish rebels crushed.

Only lasting happiness eluded me.
Yoked to a tart-tongued wife;
love swallowed by the sea's cold throat.

In the end, what matters?
Have I won? Failed
suicide, forced to let a faulty heart
choose my last hour,
I have an empire, an army,
but no partner in my bed, no son
to give my crown.

Marble Bust of a Girl

Wide-eyed girl, who were you?
Which parent gave you
such high cheekbones,
pointy chin, smooth
waves of hair cresting into
a widow's peak?

Your set lips make you
sad, or serious, a gravity
that suits someone far older
than your face implies.

Were you the sculptor's daughter,
forced to pose so he could
hone his craft? Or the child
of someone important, marked
for immortality because of blood?

Perhaps doting parents saved
to have your likeness carved,
something they could keep
when you were married off
and gone. Imagine
how they'd smile now to see you
in the company of emperors and gods.

Epicurus

The placid sea,
smoothed by the moon's
cool hands,
            is happiness.

Do not waste your prayers
        on indifferent gods.

Particles move. Swerve.
            Collide.

    If trees thrive
                or blight leaves a grove of rot,
        don't think "reward" or "punishment."

The trained mind turns from every evil
        felt as pain.

Share ripe figs and conversation
            as a mellow breeze spreads
                        birdsong through the air.

Let fears wash away
        like pebbles down a hill.
            Let friends blossom in the garden of your life.

Here our highest good is pleasure.
            Here even slaves and women
                can be free.

Death can cause
                no suffering—
the soul
        and the body
                    end as one.

This cracked, smiling statue
        teaches: *I was not; I was;*
                I am not; I do not care.

Trajan

The blue moon over Rome's congenial
as my round face, and as beloved.

It is no harder to rule wisely
than to bungle, to let

arrogance turn Rome
into a toothless mouth, an emporer's life

fodder for catty scribes.
No shame in stroking senators,

letting flattery kill opposition
more effectively than any sword. No harm

in giving common people
acrobats and bread.

See the vanquished bowing to my power.
See the Forum rising toward the stars.

If my last conquered provinces are waves—
easy to grab, refusing

to be held—no one will blame me.
And if I, the son of two strong fathers,

have no heir and leave my wife to choose,
why wouldn't history forgive?

See my marble face— its features
generously polished by the years.

Endymion Looks up at the Moon

What did I learn from that time?
That hunger leads to

more hunger, desire to mourning.
That what begins in joy

can sour to tenacity.
That there is valor in surrender.

I was young, mistook her lust
for devotion.

She enchanted me,
then turned dark and left me on the ground.

Years lost, looks gone,
I dragged myself up.

I live again
in the village. My latest

girlfriend's pretty, clever, kind.
We won't marry.

I'm wed to the memory
of bliss outside of life or death,

silver kisses no mere
human lips can match.

Pandora

I'm a hot mess, ravishing
disaster, blown into town
under a blade-sharp moon.
Men, you quiver as I slink by
with my lipsticked smirk and box
of troubles, ache at the sway
of my skirt. You've never seen
a woman's hips before, never touched hair
soft as ash. My fingers and dismissals
burn like stolen fire, punishment
so sweet you can't tell if I entered
through the ivory gate for false dreams
or the carved horn gate for true.

Athlete

Half-smirk, sweat-band to collect
my nectar. One hand
on my stone ocean of curls.
I'm blessed, loved, favored, plucked
from the mundane to dwell
in a realm between Olympus and Earth.

See me run, throw, kick—
my skill far greater grace
than wisdom or a noble heart.
Who cares about the heart—common
clump of muscle with its quotidian beat.
If I hit women, torture dogs, still
my god-given glamour dazzles.
Everything's forgiven when I win.

"Rape on Campuses isn't always because People are Rapists"

A woman's body is a pool.
                    Jump in. Splash around.

            His trophies. His scholarship. His mile time.
                The quality of his character.

                        a big ribeye steak to grill

Dirt in the hair
            Blue paint in the vagina to check for abrasions.

Brock is absolutely devastated.

A male athlete's future
                    is a banner—
                                Unfurled. Waved

            necklace wrapped around the neck
        limbs limp in the dark

                        like a woman drowned

You don't know me but you've been inside me

    Fingers   Pine needles   Debris

He had an erection because it was cold.

                        behind a dumpster

64

She was not moving, while he was moving a lot

A woman's past is a garden.
      So much to smell,
               to pluck and place on display

                     (the danger of alcohol and promiscuity)

How much do you weigh?
How much did you drink?
But where exactly?
What were you wearing?
Where did you urinate?
Would you cheat?

If a girl falls, help her up.

                    twenty minutes of action

Brock's life has been deeply altered forever.

my work, my privacy, my energy, my time,
my safety, my intimacy, my confidence, my own voice

She was enjoying it.

I don't want my body anymore.

Reeva Steenkamp

Cameras adore his chiseled face, all
symmetry and shadows. He sobs
about waking from nightmares,
won't look at the picture
of what used to be my head.

Newspapers and magazines
resell his myth.
Me they confuse with Nicole
Brown, Bonnie Bakley, Natalie Wood.
Only my mother, granite-faced
in the front row, knows
my nickname, my favorite song.

He swears that when I went
to bed that night, I felt loved.
Whether the judge buys it or not,
he'll make the history books. I'm just
the dead girl, forgettable,
common as a shoe.

Gabby Douglas

More than a hand
not pressed obediently to a heart.
More even than my muscled ass
remaining seated when my teammates soared.

My purple-lipsticked pout.
My messy (read "Black") hair.
My face
honest with disappointment.

Our country's odd monogamy—
every four years, just one sweetheart.

Fans reach out
to push me down the slide
from heroine to has-been.

Like a saggy actress, my crime's
being visible past my prime, forcing
the public to confront (their own)
diminishment.

If I were a white boy
I'd get drunk and piss against a wall,
then growl I was robbed.

Americans don't want to know
that medals can't
repair a fractured country,
that flying squirrels
don't really fly.

Arm around the new star,
I smile and pose,
gold around my neck like a rope.

Medusa

It beats invisibility,
the hell of insignificance
most women are dismissed to
when their prettiness fades.
Evil has its own loveliness.

Though I'm lonely,
life is not without pleasure—
wine by the fire, a cat
in my lap. Outside, on my neat
lawn, stone men line up like suitors.

Not Fair

I'd lived by my looks, glass-gazing
the way a man might stare
at something valuable he made,
anxiously alert for flaws.

Still, the first lines were a shock.
When bags and blotches
came, I fought—
crèmes, paints, powders,
even a brief spell
of tape behind my ears to lift the droop.

My step-daughter made it worse,
parading by with her shelf-high ass,
skin poreless as glass. Oblivious,
as I had been,
to the poison of the gift.

My howls shook the castle walls.
Left me even puffier.

Once I was beautiful;
now I am myself.

To the west, the forest,
thick with mystery.
To the east, the road
that winds around the village
and beyond.

I turned from the mirror.

Pretty Little Pantoum

Many characters kill people
in the show I watch with my daughter.
What is this teaching her?
The men take their shirts off, often.

In this show I watch with my daughter,
the star got fat but wasn't fired.
Women took their shirts off, often,
when I was growing up;

a star who got fat would get fired.
The dork with bad hair and glasses,
just like when I was growing up,
transforms easily to beautiful.

The former dork-with-bad-hair-and-glasses
is held prisoner in an underground bunker.
Despite her transformation to beautiful,
she's an outsider, desperate for friends.

Keeping prisoners in an underground bunker,
an unbalanced twin impersonates her sister.
She's an outsider, desperate for friends.
Much of the story takes place in the past.

Unbalanced twins impersonate their sisters.
Just like in real life,
much of the story takes place in the past.
The girls rescue each other.

Just like in real life,
everyone is hiding something.
The girls rescue each other—
is this a feminist statement?

Everyone's hiding something.
Lovers end up dead, or engaged.
Is it a feminist statement
that the heroines are resourceful and smart?

Lovers end up dead or engaged.
What is this teaching our daughters?
Though the heroines are resourceful and smart,
most of them kill people.

Reserves

Try not to think about buttons
you'll never sew back on,
shoved in a drawer's corner
next to an assortment of keys,
whatever they open long discarded.
Push aside images of elephants—
in circuses or slaughtered in the YA book
you read to bond with your daughter,
more violent than you'd expected, the war then
so much like the wars now. Also avoid thoughts
of your worst mistakes, and the questions
your daughter will ask, perhaps soon.
Don't dwell but practice,
your neutral face perfected,
the lies lined up like soldiers.

Caligula

If I'm not safe,
no one is safe.

My meat poisoned;
now, like rain, let blood
wash clean the streets of Rome.

Little Soldier Boot, my ass.
No part of me is small.
Only a fool
can't see I am a god.

Sisters, lovers, rivals, senators—

So many ways
to make a body tremble.
So many little deaths.

Though if I Hurt Myself Doing it, at least I Still have Health Insurance
(Rondeau with a Line by Anthony Scarmucci)

I'm not here to suck my own cock,
or yours either,
though the idea of pleasure
at will is appealing.
I'm not here,
often, when you think I am, stuck
in ideas or desires or the past.
For years I thought Johnny Thunders sang
I don't need society to open up my fly for me,
but it was *life.*
I have no problem with my pants,
many with my life. Still, distracting
though it would be (who doesn't need distraction?),
I'm not here to suck my own cock.

Endymion Explains

Though myth makes me a victim—
future stolen,
parents holy with grief—
I was the one
to offer up my body to the moon.
Burning with adolescence, I breathed
night air and longed to be the field
stroked by her beams.

Have you ever hugged oblivion?
Pleasure rushing into every cell,
fear and yearning smoothed away.
Each cracked thing made whole.

But not really.
Morning sun's harsh gold
finds me abandoned, life reduced
to lying splayed on dew-damp ground.
Laughter of the village girls like little slaps.
The foul moon tightening her hold.

Once Upon a Time

I was gullible, a trapped-
in-the-tower type,
waiting for rescue.
I ate each offered apple,
practiced dancing with a mop,
grew my hair to a climbable braid.
Nothing.
Feet scrunched into tight shoes,
I slept for days at a time.
Woke grumpy and doped.
Threw a ball into the pond
and puckered up.
No clomp of hoof beats,
no prince with magic lips
and an engagement ring.
I tossed crumbs through the bars
to draw the dragon, pricked my finger
on anything sharp I could find. Scrawled
a plea in blood on the castle wall:
My heart is oyster tender.
Take me now.
Still nothing.
Finally, axe in my teeth,
I chopped off my hands, sure
when I was patient, punished
long enough, he'd have to come.

Julia Mamaea

One dead, one drunk and thick-fingered
beside me—a husband's a weak
star to journey by.

A wife's a bauble—dropped
in a pocket, taken
from table to shelf.

But a mother! From his first flutter
at my core, I knew myself
the vessel for an emperor.

My dumpling, my duck,
my luscious flower. I fed
and fattened on each lullaby,
each milk-blue hour.

A pretty bride's a fever.
Sick with her,
he turned,

but in the end,
I triumphed. It was
my body he clung to

as the traitors raised their swords.
My screamed name
his final prayer.

Nativity

A mother and child are one.
A father's peripheral.
A walk-on role. A satellite.

I'm twice a cuckold—
first when she learned
she'd carry someone else's baby,

again when she pushed him
from her core.
I'll say what no one else admits—

he was a homely kid,
the even features he's depicted with
a shared artists' lie.

Most painters show me in shadow,
if at all, kneeling to the side
or standing with the animals.

My rage hidden behind
a bland mask. She gazes at the boy
with love and awe,

their faces glowing gold.
Her eyes glossy, drunk with him.
His mouth on her breast.

Vivia Sabina

I was still half child,
barely past first blood.
My aunt ordered me to wed.

No soft words, no tender
kisses to ease the awkward
joining of strangers.
He grated on me like rough cloth.
Fortunately he travelled.

Once I knew man-woman joy.
Suetonius and I shared humor, locked
eyes when we spoke.
Hadrian dismissed him, then went back
to his pretty boy.

Unwanted wife, mere footnote.
Still, in the end, I won.
Drank herbs bought
and brewed in secret.
Rid my body of his son.

A Dainaid Sets the Record Straight

We didn't kill our husbands—
we adored them. Saw beneath
their brutish manners
to the hurt boys they really were.
Forgave the selfishness and slaps.

Devotion's bitches, we changed
our hair. Bought lingerie. Baked
pies. Believed that understanding
could heal anything.

We grew thinner. Pale.
Forgot hobbies and friends.
Our names.

Now we drift, weak and weeping,
through marital hell, pouring
our love into broken men, watching it
leak out through the holes.

Aphrodite

Skimmed like cream from the sea, I came
with curves and symmetry, with birdsong
laughter, jeweled combs in my nacre hair.
Came with gifts of zing, jolt, dazzle, thrill.

Not endurance—time's quotidian grind,
marriage's cold noose
around the finger. Not fidelity,
that dour maiden aunt.

I give love in its unfettered
glory—*wow, yes*, gratitude
of captivated hearts, of bodies'
truest hungers felt, and filled.

Life continues.
Work, war, vendors'
sing-song at the marketplace.
Olives ripen on familiar trees.

Yet each surface of this known
world sparkles with a patina of gold,
beauty that has always shone, unnoticed.
Now, your eyes are open
and you see.

Beyond

I don't know what sex is
beyond the obvious—tension reliever,
survival drive, evolutionary necessity.
Marital glue. So what's this thing
that happens sometimes—no more
boundary, my skin dissolving
even as it burns? No way to predict it—
no special room, position, music. Our
usual bodies. What lifts us
past the realm of pleasure
into some sacred other place?

Dionysus

Only those with wine-bright eyes
        can tolerate the gods'
                full splendor,
        can kiss fire
                and not burn.

                (A sober mother
                incinerated by her lover's dazzle.

                A still-grieving teen discovering
                the cool grapes' soothing blur.)

Let frenzy
        replace sacrifice
        and somber prayer.

                Every soul seeks ecstasy.
                Everyone has something to forget.

Drain your goblets in my name
        and dance the wavy line
                between oblivion and rapture.

Let the words to every song be *yes*.

Alcoholic Cento

A suitcase is what a father carries
circulating between piano bars and cabarets
to see facts eat our dreams, our presumptions,
knives lying around, waiting
and everyone's sleeping. This is the past
Lake over fire: molting, an animal's pelt
The moon is stuck flat

The real story comes after,
Violent lighting white on the white lawn.
I believed in lies, now I believe in the sun.
Now that death has fled these quiet corridors
I have to think of excuses
I am so afraid of telling them
What it is to be human.

Endymion, Wakened

I came back to find the flock
sold, my parents old and feeble,
farm in ruins. My muscles flabby
from disuse. Everything spoiled.

Girls who used to flirt
now dropped their eyes or squeezed
their boyfriends' hands.
Matrons clutched their bags.

Pity-hired by a neighbor
to watch his sheep, I wouldn't
stop the wolves. They, too,
have been loved by the moon.

Over time, it's gotten easier.
The cravings come
less often. I go to bed early,
draw dark shades to block her beams.

Still, when full, she spills
into my dreams and finds me
anywhere I hide, binds me
with silver kisses, silver chords.

Homer

Eyes pond-cloudy, still I see
waves rock ships packed with soldiers,
an old mongrel rise
to greet his ragged master,
a boy-hero held by the heel.

I know how a shade's voice
trembles toward a living visitor,
the arc blood makes when
blade meets neck,
how an abandoned priestess burns.

I know also when a story
needs stretching, the truth
too dull to endure—Helen,
cute but not dazzling, Scylla
and Charybdis, merely rock.
I know which rhythms
turn even a tale of slaughter sweet.

Some scholars argue me unreal,
claim that no illiterate
could press words hard enough
to sparkle, declare my epics
stanzas glued together from a pack of bards.

They don't see
a man inhabited by music
doesn't have to read
to remember,
doesn't need to write to sing.

Heretic

I never got the point of God,
far-away father with his tantrums
and commandments, magic
enough to fix any problem
but usually choosing not to.
Trying to believe, I memorized
the prayers, sang what I was taught,
searched bible stories for things to like—
the ark's zoo of neatly paired animals,
the Red Sea opening like a book.

Job was my last straw.
Not a sinner, not punished,
just tortured so God could
prove something to Satan, a minor
character Jews don't even
give a place to live.

Livelihood gone, children killed,
Job stayed loyal until, pain-dazed,
he asked why, then was
berated for daring to question.
Still, it's taught as a story
that ends happily—
more animals, new kids,
his boil-scarred skin soothed,

just like the time I pushed the dresser
against my bedroom door,
my brother in one of his fits,
yelling threats, trying to pick the lock
with a screwdriver, then turning
his rage on my dolls, and afterwards
my parents buying me new ones
as though that made everything all right.

Wounded Amazon

A woman is more than her injuries

what enters
what draws blood

To fight means to be safe

to live

Most men have two faces

so an axe

needs two sharp sides

There are many kinds of wounds

In other lands my sisters

toil and spin,

men's habits, hungers

written into law

The exhilaration of a well-placed blade!

Once a warrior has killed a man in battle

she can marry

Sculpture of Alexander the Great as Young Hercules

What is a man
if not a warrior?

Battle purifies,
commands the heart to pound
its fullest,
burns off everything
but character.

My father conquered
the unguarded bodies
of women,
left Mother and me
to make our own kingdom.

Now, moon-full, my wife
ripens with our son.
King of the Four Quarters of the World,
greater fighter than the half-god heroes
of my childhood books,
I widen every boundary, dead fears
draped around me like a pelt.

Bust of a Youth

Even-featured, smug as a rock
star, what's the tale your blank
eyes hide? Were you the forced
or willing boy-toy
of a senator? A soldier?

Or did the sculptor himself
fancy you, pull from marble
full lips and lush curls
he'd later stroke?
Perhaps you were

irrelevant, the artist
driven by the muse,
any model just a means
to join the gods by breathing
life into a slab of stone.

Penelope's Confession

This isn't loyalty.
Yes, I miss kissing him
but not his boring stories
or the snoring
that fractured my dreams.

Afternoons at the loom,
my fingers transform into pictures
luscious blues, sun-yellow, tender green.
Power flowing through me like breath.

No more cramming art
into snatched moments
between cleaning and sex.

True, the nightly unmaking
stings, beauty unraveling
like a marriage, while I long
to let my work be savored
by admiring eyes.

Even with this sour compromise,
I'm greater than I've ever been,
a vessel of the gods
as much as any warrior or sage.

Matilda the Younger

Gone, my nose's bump,
my bottom lip's uneven curl.
"Idealized," I could be anyone.

True, my moonward gaze suits fashion,
but it also mirrors the artist's grumpiness
at having to sculpt me, rather than
some more important royal.

I'll be immortalized as *sister of*,
the lowest rung on
fame's bright ladder.
Worse than *wife*.

Still, don't pity me. Better
to be trivial than to let the shame
of an unloving husband
titillate the gossips of Rome.

Look closer—
though the mouth's been
altered, this half smirk's all mine.

Let Sabina stick her envied neck out.
I'll enjoy friendship and wine,
kiss whom I choose. Unwatched,
undocumented. Safe in my anonymous skin.

Frozen

I. Sisters

It's always the younger one who yearns.
Who offers bike riding, her best jokes,

and learns that love means hungering
outside a locked door.

Memories of shared laughter
freeze in her heart.

Rejection makes her reckless.
She chases storms, takes

rides from strangers,
believes any boy

with a slick opening line.
Ends up numb beside a dying fire,

dumb to the futility of fantasy,
the cad behind the kiss.

II. Elsa in Translation

Let go now
Let go and forget
Suddenly
I have this power
I will rise at dawn
I'll put it out
It wants to fly
Freed, released
I come to life
I'm letting everything go
I'm putting an end
Break free
Let it go as I am
I'm free
And I forget
Lock of the icy heart
Forget everything
It's left behind
It ends now
Doesn't matter
Don't mind it
It has already passed
Step ahead
Let it happen
Set it free
Let it go
Let it be
Let it snow

III. Finally a Fairy Tale

for all the gifted girls,
forced to hide
because our power threatens.
Guilty, hidden, cold, so lonely
we'll try anything—
conceal, don't feel—the soul-
dulling mantra that promises
a place at the dance.

Let us take off our gloves.
Conjure stairs,
then climb them.
Let our secrets
sculpt themselves from ice as weak men
cower and each flagrant note
of *Now they know* soars
from our open throats.

Let us be cold
as we need to be.
Suss the pretty prince
for what he is.
Whip up palaces and skating rinks.
When our sisters stumble,
let us take their hands
and guide them into glide.

Cinderella

People think it was the prince who mattered,
that my heart fluttered predictably at his touch.
Sure I flirted—what girl wouldn't
trade an ash heap for a feather bed?
He was nice enough, bland-cute, eager
to please. I could overlook
his weak chin, the corny jokes
he stole from the Fool.

I shone and smiled at the altar
but what I longed for
eluded me—my stepmother's razor face
gone soft, her eyes moist
as she saw me in my gown, said *beautiful,*
said *mine.*

Antinoos

Some say it was an accident—
wine-dulled I leaned too far
admiring the full moon's twin.
Fell into the Nile's open mouth.

Others claim suicide.
My face's softness gone,
my body broadening, they believe
Hadrian found a prettier boy
and sorrow drove me to dive.

A few whisper that he
had me killed. No longer desired,
I had years
that could be transferred.

Truth is, I gave willingly,
glad to feed life to my emperor,
just as he took
morsels of the night's most tender
meat and placed them on my tongue.

Yes, he hinted, cursing
his declining health while stroking
the strong muscles of my back,
telling stories of heroes
rewarded for sacrifice.

I understood. Alive, I was
replaceable.
Dead, I'd transform to a god.
I kissed him lightly, neatly
folded my clothes,
then dove into the silence.

Sorry, Perseus,

but my Medusa triumphs.
Designer shades and sword-sharp
cheekbones, a seething mass of curls—
she's the "It-girl," often snapped
gliding from a club at 3 AM, front-page
for her fling with a volatile rocker.
He hasn't been seen in weeks.
Tabloids speculate he snuck away to rehab
or to some exotic island with the maid.

Bra strap askew, crimson
lipstick smeared, Medusa
hails a cab with one green-gloved hand.
She swings her leather boots onto the seat,
stares at the back of the driver's head
as she recalls her ex's stony expression
when she left. No more
Please, Babe, one more chance.
No more shame about the changes
to her face. No more, the sour twisting
of victimhood. That story
ended when she opened her eyes.

Notes

Many of these poems were inspired by sculptures in the New York Metropolitan Museum of Art and The National Museum of Rome.

After the Mountains, More Mountains is for Linda Alcorace.

Vashti—In Jewish mythology, Vashti was a queen, banished (or killed, depending on the version) for refusing to dance naked at her husband's party.

Demosthenes—Athenian orator (384–322 BCE). Lines 17-19 and 25-27 borrow from, and alter, lines from Third Philippic, 69.

Hermes—Hermes angered Apollo by stealing his heard of cattle. He calmed the god's wrath by inventing a musical instrument from a turtle's shell.

Statue of Caracalla—Caracalla was responsible for his brother's murder. He also betrayed his planned father-in-law by having soldiers attack during the wedding; his bride was killed. The structure of this poem is influenced by Richard Siken's poem, Landscape with Several Small Fires.

Hadrian—The first two lines come from a poem by Hadrian: "Little soul, wandering and pale, guest and companion of my body, you who will now go off to places pale, stiff, and barren, nor will you
make jokes as had been your wont."

Epicurus—Line 21 is a variation of the inscription on the gate to the Garden: "Stranger, here you will do well to tarry; here our highest good is pleasure." The last two lines quote the Epicurean epitaph.

Report—In December, 2017, a CDC employee reported that Donald Trump had forbidden (the language was later changed to "discouraged") use of the italicized words in official documents.

Prom Night—Line 27 quotes a lyric from Patti Smith's "Gloria."

"Rape on Campus isn't always because People are Rapists"—On January 8, 2015, Stanford student Brock Turner was interrupted raping an unconscious woman behind a dumpster. Initial news coverage focused on his swimming prowess rather than the crime. The title and other italicized lines in smaller font are quotes from Turner's parents and friend, as well as one of the men who interrupted the rape. The italicized questions are among those the victim was asked. Phrases in larger type are from a letter she read at the trial.

Reeva Steenkamp—Steenkamp was shot to death by her partner, Paralympic athlete Oscar Pistorius, who claimed he mistook her for an intruder.

Gabby Douglas—Olympic Gymnast, nicknamed "The Flying Squirrel." Douglas was blasted on social media during the 2016 games. During the same games, swimmer Ryan Lochte drunkenly vandalized a convenient store and concocted a story about being robbed at gunpoint.

Not Fair—The italicized lines are by Anne Sexton.

Pretty Little Pantoum—Based on the TV show "Pretty Little Liars."

Caligula—Though mostly remembered for his debauchery and cruelty, by many accounts he was a fair and just ruler until an incident of food poisoning, which may or may not have been deliberate.

Though if I Hurt Myself Doing it, at Least I Still have Health Insurance—Anthony Scaramucci, Donald Trump's Communications Director for ten days, told a New York Times reporter, "Unlike Steve Bannon, I'm not here to suck my own cock."

Alcoholic Cento—Comprised of lines from the anthology, *Last Call*, Sarah Gorham and Jeffrey Skinner, eds. (Sarabande Books, 1997).

Frozen—Based on the 2013 Disney movie. Section II is made from the title of the song "Let it Go" as it was translated into other languages and then back to English.

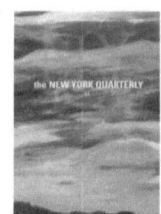